A Great White Christmas

Written & Illustrated by
Cody VandeZande

For Dominic!

Cody VandeZande

It was Christmas Eve morning at the North Pole
and everyone was busy preparing for Santa's big night.

The elves in Santa's workshop worked hard down to the last minute. They were putting the finishing touches on the last few gifts with ribbons and bows before sending them out to the sleigh.

N. POLE

All of the elves were busy that day. Some loaded gifts on the sleigh and checked the gadgets while others were in charge of rounding up the reindeer.

Mrs. Claus worked hard all day preparing Santa's favorite dinner.

Is everything ready to go for tonight, dear?

Everyone came out to see Santa off. They shouted and cheered as he called each reindeer by name. Mrs. Claus blew him kisses as they flew out of sight.

Shortly after the journey began, they encountered some
trouble when Santa received a message on the radar.
"ALERT! A huge windstorm over parts of Australia!"

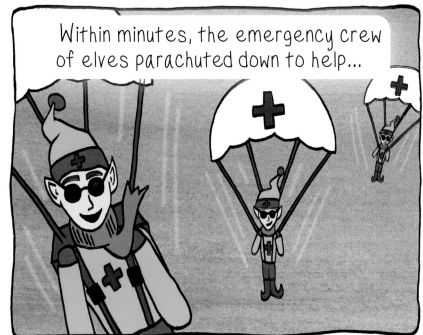

While the kangaroos and koalas delivered gifts to the houses inland, Santa and Oli delivered gifts to each house along the shoreline with a high-tech gift launcher that was hidden in the sleigh.

Everyone was happy and excited that things were back on track! Until...

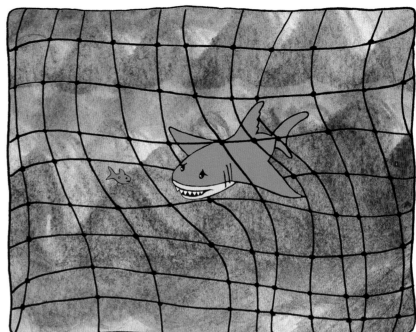

Santa called out, "Merry Christmas!" to his new friends.
Oli watched as they flew away and felt happy that he helped save Christmas.

ATTENTION: DID YOU KNOW?

*Because of the movies and humans, sharks have a bad reputation.

*Sharks keep our ecosystem balanced, which allows for a healthy and livable environment for us humans on Earth.

*They are incredibly intelligent animals that have been around longer than the dinosaurs!

*There are more than 500 species of sharks and many of them are considered endangered or threatened.

Be the change!

Help save the sharks & other ocean animals from extinction!

Facts gathered from www.sharkangels.org & www.sharks-world.com

Thank you!

To each and every one of you that helped me reach the goal to get this book sent to the printer! Thank you so much! I sincerely appreciate it and am so grateful that you've helped me achieve this dream! Also, a big thank you goes to all of you who have helped me along the way of creating this book!

An extra special thank you to the following:

Jake Kazmierski
for taking me on the fantastic adventure to Australia and getting me to actually dive with great white sharks in the first place and for helping me gather up the story line for this book!

Rodney Fox Shark Expeditions
for allowing Jake and I to be a part of the amazing diving experience that started this whole idea and for everything you do with research and conservation to help protect our sharks!

John Gregg
for working with me in class to make the mere idea of *A Great White Christmas* an actuality and for the donation to help get it to the printers!

Brenna Ferguson
for helping me make the promotional video for my kickstarter campaign (and being patient when we had to do it over 100 times!) and for the donation!

Rick VandeZande
for being my dad and always supporting me, for always helping me reach my goals in life and for the generous donation to this book!

Cari VandeZande
for being my mom and always supporting me, for being the very first person to inspire me to become an artist, and thank you for the generous donation to help with my book!